Where We Live

Kenya

Donna Bailey and Anna Sproule

RAINTREE
STECK-VAUGHN
PUBLISHERS
The Steck-Vaughn Company
Austin, Texas

Hello! My name is Wanjiru.

I live in Nairobi.

Nairobi is the capital of Kenya.

These trees with purple flowers
grow everywhere in Nairobi.
They are jacaranda trees and give lots of
shade from the hot sun.

We have jacaranda trees in our garden.
There are many other flowers, too.
We often eat our meals in the garden.
This is my favorite meal, a plate of ugali.
Ugali is a thick cereal made from corn.
Everyone eats it with their fingers!

Nairobi is a busy modern city.
In the center of the city there are
many stores, banks, and offices,
as well as a big market.

My sister Wangari likes to shop
for cloth at the market.
She helps Mom make all our clothes.

In the center of Nairobi there is
a huge statue of Jomo Kenyatta.
He was the first President of Kenya and
head of our government.

Kenyan people meet their friends here. They read the newspaper and talk about the news and the government.

Every year there is a special parade in Nairobi on October 20, Kenyatta Day. The school children have a holiday, and many of them go to watch the parade.

Our school choir practices
for Kenyatta Day.
We learn special songs to sing when
we march in the parade.

People come from all over Kenya
to join in the parade.
There are many bands and groups of
dancers from different parts of the country.

These dancers from the Samburu tribe
are wearing their traditional costume.
They dance the traditional dances
of their tribe.

These drummers are from the Kikuyu tribe.
Many Kikuyu are farmers and live in
the Kenyan highlands, not far from Nairobi.
My family belongs to the Kikuyu tribe.

We often visit our relatives
on their farm.
My Uncle Njorge grows coffee, tea,
and vegetables.

My aunt helps hoe the vegetables in the fields to get rid of the weeds. Kikuyans use a special hoe called a jembe to separate the weeds from the vegetables.

My uncle has a very big tractor to
help him plow his fields.
Crops grow well in the Kenyan highlands.

When it is time to pick the tea,
all the women in the village help.
They pick the young tips of the bushes and
put the tea in the baskets on their backs.
The tea leaves are dried and
packed to send to other countries.

Traditional Kikuyu houses are round and
have thatched roofs.
The walls are made of straw and mud bricks
that have been baked in the sun.

The roofs are thatched with grass or reeds. The thatch keeps the houses cool, even in the hottest weather.

These people are from the Ilchamus tribe.
They live in a fishing village on
the shores of Lake Baringo.

People in the Ilchamus tribe make a framework of poles for their houses. Then they build up the walls and thatch the roof.

When they have finished, the Ilchamus might decorate their houses with patterns.

This young girl is from the Masai tribe.
She is wearing many bead necklaces.
The Masai make bracelets, necklaces, and
belts from colorful beads.

The Masai people care for large
herds of cattle.
Their cattle roam the grasslands of
Masai Mara in southwestern Kenya.

The young boys herd the cattle.
During the dry season, the Masai move
from place to place to find fresh grass
for their cattle to eat.

The women milk the cows and make cheese.
The Masai drink cow's blood mixed with
milk to make them strong.

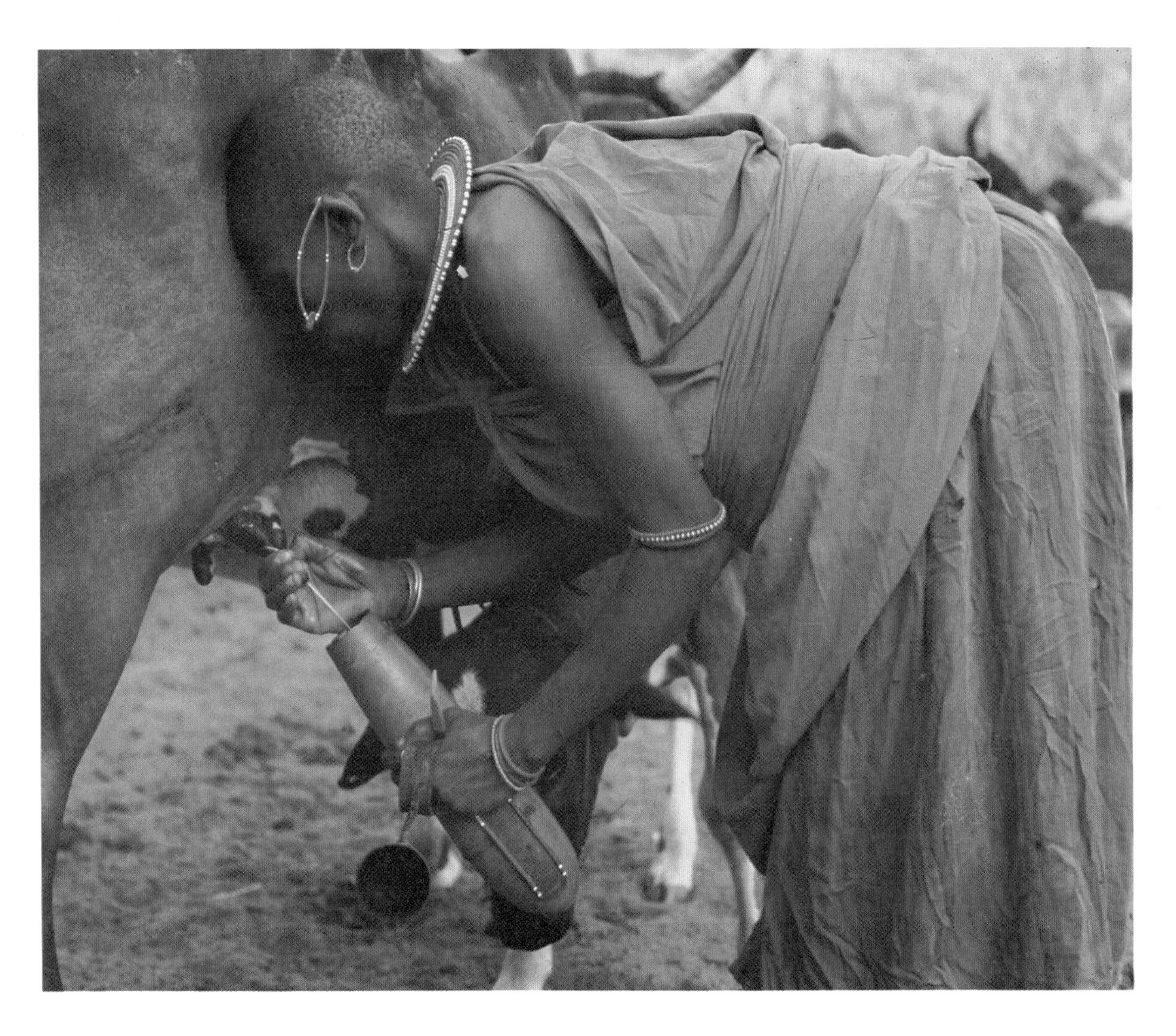

These men are warriors of the Masai tribe.
They grow their hair very long.
They color their hair with a red dye called
ocher, then braid it into long, thin strands.

Masai warriors are very tall.
They wear bead necklaces and carry
shields and spears.
When they dance together, they leap
high into the air.

Many tourists come to Kenya
to see the animals in
Kenya's famous national parks.
The tourists travel through the parks in
small trucks and vans.

You can see many animals
in the national parks.
These monkeys and zebras are in
the Nairobi National Park.

Tourists like to take photographs
of all the wild animals.
This woman is taking a photograph
of a rhinoceros.
Rhinos can be dangerous animals, especially
when they get angry and charge at you.

There are not many rhinos left in some
of the national parks.
Animal poachers have killed so many
rhinos for their horns that rhinos are now
in danger of dying out.

Index

Reading Consultant: Diana Bentley
Editorial Consultant: Donna Bailey
Executive Editor: Elizabeth Strauss
Project Editor: Becky Ward

Picture research by Jennifer Garratt
Designed by Richard Garratt Design

Photographs
Cover: © Norman Myers / Bruce Coleman, Inc.
Adams Picture Library: 2 (Betram Davis), 6 (J. Grey)
Camerapix Picture Library: title page, 3,5,9,11,30
Colorific Photo Library: 13 (Tony Carr), 15 (Mary Fisher), 16,17 (John Moss), 18 (Terence Spencer), 25 (Mirelle Ricciardi), 31 (Ben Martin)
Douglas Dickens FRPS: 29
The Hutchison Library: 4 (Liba Taylor), 8 (Timothy Beddow) 7,14
OSF Picture Library: 19 (David Shale), 20,21,22 (David Cayless), 26 (Edwin Sadd), 32 (Mike Birkhead)
Robert Harding Picture Library: 10,12,23,24,27,28

Library of Congress Cataloging-in-Publication Data: Bailey, Donna. Kenya / Donna Bailey and Anna Sproule. p. cm.—(Where we live) SUMMARY: A child living in Nairobi describes the daily life, housing, agriculture, people, and parks of Kenya. ISBN 0-8114-2563-0 1. Kenya—Social life and customs—Juvenile literature. 2. Nairobi (Kenya)—Social life and customs—Juvenile literature. 3. Masai (African people)—Social life and customs—Juvenile literature. [1. Kenya—Social life and customs.] I. Sproule, Anna. II. Title. III. Series: Bailey, Donna. Where we live. DT433.54.B35 1990 967.62—dc20 90-9644 CIP AC

Trade Edition published 1992 © Steck-Vaughn Company

ISBN 0-8114-2563-0 hardcover library binding ISBN 0-8114-7178-0 softcover binding

3 4 5 6 7 8 9 LB 96 95